God Gave Us Prayer

by Lisa Tawn Bergren   art by David Hohn

WATERBROOK

For Celeste and Vivian:
May you know the joy of talking
with our God who loves you,
all your life long!

Love, "Auntie" Lisa

God Gave Us Prayer

Copyright © 2021 by Lisa Tawn Bergren
Illustrations copyright © 2021 by David Hohn

All rights reserved.

Published in the United States by WaterBrook, an imprint of Random House, a division of Penguin Random House LLC.

WaterBrook® and its deer colophon are registered trademarks of Penguin Random House LLC.

ISBN 978-0-525-65411-7
Ebook ISBN 978-0-525-65412-4

The Library of Congress catalog record is available at https://lccn.loc.gov/2020019515.

Printed in the United States of America

waterbrookmultnomah.com

10 9 8 7 6 5 4 3 2 1

First Edition

Book and cover design by Annalisa Sheldahl
Cover illustrations by David Hohn

Special Sales Most WaterBrook books are available at special quantity discounts when purchased in bulk by corporations, organizations, and special-interest groups. Custom imprinting or excerpting can also be done to fit special needs. For information, please email specialmarketscms@penguinrandomhouse.com.

"Whatcha doin' out here, Mama?"
Little Pup asked, plopping
down beside her.

"I'm spending some time with God,
Little Pup. Praying."

"Huh? I don't see your lips moving."

Mama smiled. "Well, God is an amazing listener,"
she said. "He can hear our prayers,
even when they're *thoughts*."

"How can God hear our thoughts?"
Little Pup asked.

"Well, God made us. He made our bodies and
our minds. He knows every part of us! So we
can speak to him silently or whisper . . ."

"Or shout?" Little Pup yelled.

"Or shout," Mama said with a giggle.
"Or sing. No matter how we pray,
God hears us."

"Can he hear us when
we're upside down?"

"Yes, he can. Or right side
up. Or sideways. Or even
when we're doing cartwheels."

"Weird!" Little Pup said.
"But what do you say to him?"

"I often tell God how much
I love and appreciate him."

"How would I do that?"

"Here's one way you could tell him: 'God, thank you for being my God. For caring about little me—along with so many others—in this big beautiful world! Thank you for loving me and blessing my life. Amen.'"

"Is that the only reason God gave us prayer?
To tell him how much we love him?"

"It's a good reason, but not the only one.
I also need to tell him the things I've done
wrong and the things I *should* have done
but didn't. We call that confession."

"Does God get mad at us when we mess up?"

"No matter what we do, God loves us and wants
us to do what's best, which is obey him. But when
we don't, we need to tell God we're sorry. And we
know we're forgiven because Jesus died for us."

"Will he forgive me for *all* my bad choices?"

"Absolutely. If you ask him to."

Little Pup got quiet. "Even for stealing
a fish out of Edgar's basket?"

Mama paused. "Yes. But you need to go tell Edgar
what you did and ask him to forgive you first."

"Oh, man. But Ed had so many!"

"That wasn't your decision, Little Pup. You could have asked him for one, right?"

"Probably," Little Pup groaned.

"We have to do our part, Little Pup.
Make things right with those we've wronged.
Even though Jesus makes things right for us in
heaven, he still asks us to try here on earth."

"But that's *hard*."

"Yes, it is. But then next time maybe
we'll remember how hard it was and
make better choices."

"How do I tell God I'm sorry?"

"You could say, 'God, I've messed up.
Help me make it right and do better in the future.
Please forgive me for my sins. Amen.'"

"And then what does God do?"

"He forgives us. It's like these sparks rising from the fire into the night and disappearing. For him, it's over and done."

"God doesn't remember the next morning? Or the next week?"

"Nope. He washes us clean. He lets us start fresh!"

"That's cool of God."

"Yes, it is. It's one of the many reasons we can be glad that God gave us prayer."

"Today what would you thank God for, Little Pup?"

He grinned. "Well, for fresh fish for my lunch . . ."

"And friends who will probably forgive you," she said,
nudging him. "How 'bout thanking him now with a real prayer?"

"While we're walking? With our eyes open and everything?"

"With our eyes open and everything."

"Well, okay," he said. "Thank you, God, for friends who *hopefully* forgive us, for climbing trees, for mountain hikes with my mama, and for bonfires."

"And thank you, Father, that we can come to you with anything," Mama added. "Good things and bad things. And that you love us, no matter what. Amen."

"Thank you for my papa, waiting for us at night!"
Little Pup said, leaping into his papa's arms.

"And our cozy home," Mama said.

"Are we praying?" Papa asked with a smile.

"Yes! With our eyes open and everything!" Little Pup said.

"Well, then," Papa said, "thank you, Lord,
for bringing my family back safe and sound.
And thanks that we can *finally* have dinner. Amen."

"Do you pray every day, Papa?"
Little Pup asked. "Like Mama does?"

"Every day, all through the day," Papa said.
"God gave us prayer so we could talk to him whenever
we want! And talking to him makes me feel closer to him."

"What do you pray for?"

"Well, often I pray for what I need
or you need or Mama needs.
Or what our friends and
pack might need."

"I want a new Super Wolf action figure!
Think God could give me that?"

"It's not really *stuff* I ask for, Little Pup.
Today I asked God to heal Molly the Moose's leg.
I prayed that the Goose family can build a new nest
after the big storm. And that God would bring
you and Mama safely home to me."

"What would you like to talk to God about today, Little Pup?"
Mama said. "Think of others as well as yourself. It's your turn."

"Okay," he said. "Dear God, please help me be brave when
I talk to Edgar tomorrow, and help him see I'm really sorry.
Heal Peter the Possum's hurt tail. And help me catch
my own fish tomorrow. Amen."

"Mama," Little Pup said a few days later, "I think we have a problem . . . I kinda told everyone that you taught me how to pray. Now all my friends want to learn too."

Mama laughed. "That's not a problem! It's easy. You just talk to God about what you're thinking or feeling."

"Feeling? You mean like when I'm scared?" Little Owl asked. "How would I talk to him about that?"

"Well," Mama said, "you could say something like this . . ."

Lord, I'm little, but you are big and mighty!
Chase away my fear, and fill me with your
courage and strength. Help me know that you
and your angels are all around me. Amen.

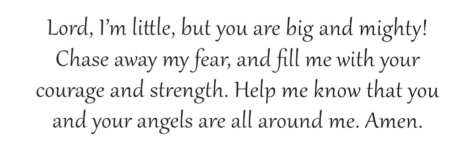

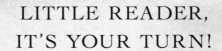

LITTLE READER,
IT'S YOUR TURN!

Have an adult help you fill in
the rest of this prayer.

Savior, I'm afraid of _____.
Help me know you're always
with me! Amen.

"Sometimes I don't know how to tell God I think he's cool," Little Skunk admitted. "I run out of words and stuff."

"That happens to me sometimes too," Mama said. "You could say something like this . . ."

Lord, you are the best, and I love you.
There is no one like you! The entire world
is your amazing creation. You made me,
and I'm so glad you're my God. Amen.

LITTLE READER,
IT'S YOUR TURN!

Creator God, I think it's awesome that
you _____. I love you and
who you are! Amen.

"What about when I'm worried?" Little Goose asked. "Sometimes I think and think about things all day!"

"Me too," Mama said. "But if we concentrate on how God is super powerful and strong, it's hard to keep worrying. You could say something like this . . ."

Father, you hold the whole world in your hands . . . including little me! You know what's in my mind and in my heart, so you know what I'm worried about. Help me let my mind rest, and help me focus on what's right in my world rather than on what's wrong. Amen.

**LITTLE READER,
IT'S YOUR TURN!**

Lord, I worry about _____.
Help me trust that you will be with me,
no matter what happens. Amen.

"Sometimes I make bad decisions," Little Otter said.
"And I'm too shy to tell God about it."

"I understand that," Mama said.
"You could say something like this . . ."

Lord, I'm sorry. Please forgive me for the ways I've failed others. For not telling the truth. For not always being nice. For getting cranky. For not helping or listening. Please help me make better decisions. Amen.

LITTLE READER, IT'S YOUR TURN!

Jesus, I'm sorry for _____. Thank you for forgiving me! Amen.

"I am soooo thankful for my family,"
Little Raccoon said. "How do I thank God for them?"

"Well," Mama said, "you could try something like this . . ."

God, thank you for surrounding me with those who love me. Help me see how their love is a little like yours. Thanks for all the fun we have together. I'm so glad I am theirs and they are mine. Amen.

LITTLE READER, IT'S YOUR TURN!

Father God, thank you for my _____. Help me always appreciate them. Amen.

"I don't like scary dreams," Little Bear said.
"Sometimes I can't get back to sleep after I have one.
Can God fix that too?"

"I don't like bad dreams either," Mama said.
"But God inspires our imaginations, which fuel
our dreams! You could pray like this . . ."

God, you created sunrises and sunsets. You are
with me throughout the day and with me as I sleep.
Help me think of all the good things in my life, not
anything scary. Protect my imagination and fill my
mind with good dreams tonight. Amen.

**LITTLE READER,
IT'S YOUR TURN!**

Lord, help me dream of those I love and happy things tonight! Like _____ and _____. Amen.

"Good grief!" Little Moose cried.
"Do you have a prayer for *everything*?"

Mama laughed. "Well, not everything. But I've been
at this awhile. The longer you walk with God
and talk with him, the easier praying becomes."

"That's true," Little Pup said. "You're pretty old."

"Have you ever not known what to pray?" Little Bear asked.

Mama thought for a moment. "Once in a while. Like when I was so surprised I couldn't even think. I had no words, only feelings. Or when I was so sad I could barely breathe. But even in those times, God can read our hearts. He knows what we're feeling and thinking before we do."

"Did that help?" Little Bear asked.
"To know he could read your heart?"

"Mmm, yes. God is the greatest comforter in my life. He can be a comfort to you too."

"What if I want to be the best student in the whole class?"
Little Pup asked.

"Yeah!" Little Otter said. "Or the best on the team?"

"Hmm," Mama said. "God doesn't care about what we do as much
as he cares about what's in our hearts. You could pray like this . . ."

*God, you created me in your image. Help me to be kind. To love and help
others. To be thankful. To smile more than frown. To speak with gentle
words. And to do my best but not have to be the best. Amen.*

LITTLE READER,
IT'S YOUR TURN!

God, I am your child, made to be
like you. Help me act more like
you by_____. Amen.

"If God knows everything," Little Pup asked,
"even what's in our hearts and minds,
why do we need to say anything at all?"

"Well, I know a lot about you, and you know a lot
about me," Mama said. "What if we never said
anything to each other? How would that feel?"

"Kinda lonely," he admitted.

"Right. God wants a relationship
with us, so he wants to hear from us!"

"Sometimes I get soooo angry
when life doesn't seem fair," Little Goose said.

"It's hard when we're feeling that way," Mama said.
"But God can help us with jealousy too.
You could pray something like this . . ."

Lord, sometimes I get jealous of others. I get angry when I have to do things that others don't. Or when others get things I want. Help me know that you have good plans for me, in your time. Give me patience as I wait and trust. Amen.

LITTLE READER, IT'S YOUR TURN!

God, I think this wasn't fair: _____. Help me know that you make all things right in time and that I don't have to. Amen.

"Right now I have all these friends," Little Skunk said.
"But sometimes I get lonely when kids don't seem to like me or when they're playing with others. How do we pray about that?"

"Friends are important," Mama said. "I'd pray like this . . ."

God, I want to make friends, but I get shy. Help me reach out to others, asking them to play. Help me not worry about those who don't want to or can't. I know you'll help me find others who will. Teach me to treat everyone I meet with kindness and love. Amen.

LITTLE READER,
IT'S YOUR TURN!

Father, when I'm lonely, help me remember that you are always with me and that you want me to _____. Amen.

"My grandma is sick," Little Moose said. "Will God help her get better if I pray?"

"Hmm, that's hard," Mama said. "But God does want us to pray for healing. You could say something like this . . ."

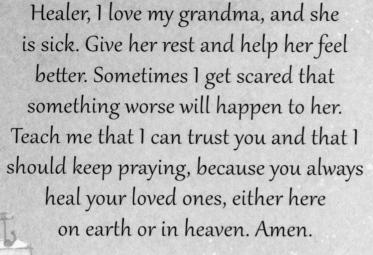

Healer, I love my grandma, and she is sick. Give her rest and help her feel better. Sometimes I get scared that something worse will happen to her. Teach me that I can trust you and that I should keep praying, because you always heal your loved ones, either here on earth or in heaven. Amen.

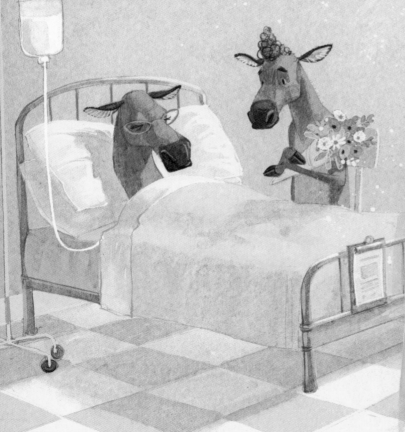

LITTLE READER, IT'S YOUR TURN!

Healing God, please help
_____, who is sick with
_____. Give them comfort
and good care and bring
them healing! Amen.

"What if we want to be more like Jesus?"
Little Bear asked. "How do we pray about that?"

"Well," Mama said, "that's a very important prayer
because he likes nothing better than when we
become more like him! I'd pray something like this . . ."

God, teach me to be more like your Son: kind and loving,
forgiving and encouraging others, thankful for everything,
and, most of all, connected to you! Amen.

LITTLE READER,
IT'S YOUR TURN!

Jesus, help me be more like you.
Especially the way you
_____. Amen.

"I'm glad that God gave us prayer, Mama," Little Pup said.

"Me too, Little Pup."

"I liked all the prayers we talked about."

"Just keep talking to him, sweet one, all the time. That's why God gave us prayer. So we could talk to him any part of the day."

"Or night!"

"Or night."

Later, when Little Pup
was cozy in his bed, he thanked God for
his life, his family, and his friends. He asked
God to forgive him and for help to make better
choices. Then he took a long deep breath and
felt God's love and peace surround him.

"Thank you for giving us prayer, God," he whispered.

And as he drifted off to sleep, he wondered
just what he might pray tomorrow.